# THE FANTASTIC FRAME

## Warning! Journey to Forever

BY **LIN OLIVER**

ILLUSTRATED BY
**EMILY KIMBELL**

BASED ON ORIGINAL CHARACTER
DESIGNS BY SAMANTHA KALLIS

Penguin Workshop

For all the children who come to the United States
to make a new home. Welcome—LO

With thanks to Daniel and the Rain Club—EK

# W

PENGUIN WORKSHOP
An Imprint of Penguin Random House LLC, New York

Penguin supports copyright. Copyright fuels creativity, encourages diverse voices,
promotes free speech, and creates a vibrant culture. Thank you for buying an authorized
edition of this book and for complying with copyright laws by not reproducing, scanning,
or distributing any part of it in any form without permission. You are supporting writers
and allowing Penguin to continue to publish books for every reader.

Text copyright © 2019 by Lin Oliver. Illustrations copyright © 2019 by
Samantha Kallis. All rights reserved. Published by Penguin Workshop,
an imprint of Penguin Random House LLC, New York. PENGUIN and
PENGUIN WORKSHOP are trademarks of Penguin Books Ltd,
and the W colophon is a registered trademark of Penguin Random House LLC.
Manufactured in China.

Visit us online at www.penguinrandomhouse.com.

Library of Congress Cataloging-in-Publication Data is available upon request.

ISBN 9781524786991 | 10 9 8 7 6 5 4 3 2 1

# PROLOGUE

Hi there. I believe we've met before.

I'm Tiger Brooks, the guy who travels with his friend Luna Lopez through a magical picture frame into great works of art. I suppose you know that our time travels only happen during the hour of power. At four o'clock, we get sucked into a painting, and if we're not back where we started at exactly five o'clock, we're stuck in the world of art forever.

That's right, I said *forever*, as in F-O-R-E-V-E-R. There's no coming back. It's not like you can call a friend and say, "I'm ready to come home now." The one thing I've learned about the world of art is that the cell phone reception there seriously stinks.

Our magical picture frame is located in our neighbor Viola Dots's house. It pulled her son, David, right out of her living room fifty years ago, and she's been searching for him in paintings ever since. Luna and I have been trying to help her find him. Don't ask me how this crazy frame got to be so magical. I don't have a clue. But I can tell you that traveling through it is a fantastic adventure.

Let me warn you, the adventure I'm going to tell you about is different from the ones before. It has, as my grandma always says, a completely new wrinkle. It's funny that my grandma loves that expression, because the last thing she needs is a new wrinkle. She already has about a million of them. She even has some on her knees, but don't tell her I told you.

I know you're not reading this to learn about knee wrinkles. You want to know why this particular adventure is so different, right? Well, here's a clue: The story is called the Journey to Forever. As in F-O-R-E-V-E-R.

So flip the page, friends, and dig in. As for me, I'll be waiting for you at the end.

# CHAPTER 1

Everything in the world was just right. It was Sunday afternoon, a soft breeze was coming through the open window, and I was at my favorite place in the world.

My invention desk.

It's just a regular desk, but it's where I work my magic. My desk is packed with all my tools, like my voltage meter and my ten-piece screwdriver kit. And I rigged up a set of containers to store all my tiny screws, washers and nuts, copper wires, microchips, and, of course, more tiny screws.

There's no place I'd rather be than sitting at my invention desk, squinting at a circuit board. It was especially great that Sunday because my chatterbox of a little sister, Maggie, was outside trying to earn some money at her lemonade stand.

I was all set to begin work on my latest invention, something I call the Pocket Buddy. It's a super-duper all-in-one tool featuring a pair of scissors, a spork, a mini magnifying glass, a little pen, and a breath-mint dispenser. Suddenly, my mom burst through the door without knocking. I hadn't even heard her footsteps coming down the hall. She'd probably taken off her shoes so she could surprise me. Moms are sneaky that way.

"Tiger, Maggie needs your help," she said.

"Didn't you read the sign on my door?"

I shot back. "No parents without prior appointment."

"It's that Cooper Starr kid," my mom said. "Actually, it's his little brother."

"You mean Pooch?"

"That sounds like a dog's name."

"It's what everyone calls Andrew Starr," I explained. "That kid's as bad as his big brother. On Friday at school, I saw him put someone's lunch box in the trash can. That's his idea of fun."

"Well, it looks like Cooper and Pooch are trying to run Maggie out of business," my mom said. "She needs your help."

"Why can't you help her?"

"Tiger, you know it's embarrassing to have your mom stick up for you. It's much cooler when your older brother does. So I'd like you to go outside and see what you can do."

I couldn't believe my ears. First, my mom burst into my room and interrupted my precious invention time. Now she was ordering me to help my little sister fight a lemonade-stand war against the Starr brothers, the biggest jerks this side of Mars.

"I don't know the first thing about lemonade stands," I said, "or even how to make lemonade. It's made from grapefruit, correct?"

"Very clever, Einstein," Mom said. "But it won't work."

"Mom, do you think Thomas Edison's mother asked him to help his little sister when he was right in the middle of inventing the lightbulb?"

"First of all, you're not inventing the

lightbulb. And second, Maggie needs help now. She wants to raise ten dollars by five o'clock so she can go to the mall with her friend Hazel's family to buy a Shop-Cool doll."

I sighed loud and long, and I let it hang in the air for a while. Oh sure, I could think of more comebacks, throw a tantrum, come down with a case of yellow fever . . . but in the end, it wouldn't matter. My mom would win.

"Knock knock" came a friendly voice from the hallway.

Luna, my upstairs neighbor, poked her head into my room.

"I heard your conversation from the porch," she said. "We'd love to help Maggie, Mrs. Brooks. My grandma always says nothing is more important than family."

"What about minding your own business?" I said. "Doesn't your grandma believe in that?"

"No," Luna said with a laugh. "Now, what are you waiting for, Tiger? We have lemonade to sell."

I sighed again. Luna is my best friend, but she might be a little too nice for this world.

"Well, Tiger?" my mom said, her hands on her hips.

"Well, Tiger?" Luna repeated, her hands on her hips, too.

That was too many hands on hips for me. I buckled under the pressure. I put away my tiny screws and headed outside.

Seemed like the world was just going to have to wait one more day for the Pocket Buddy.

# CHAPTER 2

Luna and I stepped out of our duplex into a perfect Los Angeles day. Well, it had been

perfect before everyone decided I had to go into the lemonade-selling, sister-saving business.

I checked the time on my Batman watch. After I'd left the first one behind on one of my fantastic frame journeys, my uncle Cole gave me the one off his own wrist. What a great uncle. I hope you have your own version of Uncle Cole.

According to Batman, it was 2:24 p.m.

"Let's make this quick," I said to Luna. "Maybe I can still work on my invention before the hour of power."

"That's not until four o'clock," Luna said.

"Viola said she wanted us to be there early today," I reminded her.

"Oh, right. She told us that this week's art adventure is really important."

"I wonder what that's supposed to mean," I said as we headed down the driveway to the sidewalk.

I was ready to be annoyed with Maggie, but that changed when I saw her sad little lemonade stand. She was just sitting by the table, with a pitcher of gray-looking lemonade and a stack of paper cups in front of her. There was also a fishbowl she was using to hold the money. Only there was no money in it. I really felt bad for her when I saw her wiping tears from her eyes.

"Dunnn-da-da-daaaaa," Luna sang. "We have come to save the day!"

"Oh," Maggie said, pretending as if she hadn't been crying. "Do you want to buy a cup of lemonade?"

"Not really," I said, swishing around the icky-looking lemonade with a spoon.

She'd clearly made the stuff herself. I don't know how much experience you've had with five-year-olds, but you don't want to taste any drink they've made with their own grubby hands. Their drinks usually contain a secret ingredient, and that secret ingredient is never something you should swallow, such as tiny bits of shredded paper or a spoonful of mud.

"We're here to help you get some customers for your lemonade stand," Luna said, "so you can buy the toy you want."

"Really?" Maggie's eyes lit up. "Shop-

Cool dolls are my favorite."

"First things first," Luna said to Maggie. "Let's test your lemonade."

She poured herself a cup of lemonade and brought it to her lips.

"Wait, don't!" I yelled, but it was too late.

The stuff was already in Luna's mouth. I watched as she swallowed, grabbed her neck, and tried not to throw up. Her eyes watered, and her entire mouth turned into a pucker.

"It's interesting," she said at last. "Something tells me you made it yourself?"

"Mommy squeezed the lemons, and I added the secret ingredients," Maggie confessed.

"I see," Luna said. She dipped her finger into the cup and pulled out some crumpled-up dead leaves.

"I didn't put those leaves in it," Maggie said. "It was that mean boy, Pooch. And then he set up his stand right on our street."

I looked down the block and saw the competition. There were quite a few people at Pooch's stand. He had a great sign and bags of ice, and I could see cartons of ready-made lemonade on his table. It was that sugar drink called Marty's Lem-O that's not really even lemonade. Maggie and I aren't allowed to drink it because Mom says it would make our teeth fall out.

Helping Pooch was his horrible big brother, Cooper Starr. He calls himself Super Cooper, but Luna and I think his nickname should be World's Number One Creep. He's mean, and that's on a good day.

"We'll have to make some new lemonade," Luna said. "And no offense, Maggie, but maybe we should try a different recipe. Tiger, why don't you go grab lemons from the tree in the backyard? I'll get some sugar and supplies from my house."

The low-hanging lemons had already been picked, so I had to use a fruit picker to get to the lemons on the top branches.

I picked at least fifteen lemons and took them to our porch. Then I had to squeeze them. That was hard. You don't actually squeeze very much juice from each lemon, and when you finally get some, you have to get a strainer to fish out all the seeds.

Then it hit me. I had invented a solution for this lemon-squeezing problem.

The Pocket Buddy! I had two perfectly good Pocket Buddy prototypes on my desk. (A *prototype* is what we inventor types call the early model of something we make.) I ran to my room and grabbed them both, then met Luna back on the porch. She had brought water, sugar, and a plastic pitcher from her kitchen.

"What's this?" she asked when I handed her one of the prototypes.

"The newest and best time-saving device ever invented," I bragged.

I showed her how to use the scissors to cut the lemons into wedges, and the sporks

to remove the seeds that were floating in
the juice. I had even installed a tiny FM
radio on my newest prototype. I pulled out
the antenna, and we listened to a couple of
tunes while we finished the lemonade.

When the pitcher was full, we hurried
over to Maggie's stand.

"Good news, Mags," I said, putting
the pitcher on the table. "Now we have

something great that you can sell."

"All we have to do is advertise our product," Luna said.

She ran into her house and came back with a piece of poster board and colorful markers. Luna collects art supplies the way I collect screws, bolts, and circuit boards.

"We're going to make you a big sign," Luna told Maggie. "First, we need a catchy name for your stand."

"How about Easy Peasy Lemon Squeezy?" I suggested.

Luna burst out laughing.

"But I want my name on the sign," Maggie said.

"Okay, how about Lil' Maggie's Handmade Lemonade?" Luna said.

"I'm not little," Maggie protested. "I'm big."

Luna made a colorful sign that said BIG MAGGIE'S HANDMADE LEMONADE and stood it up on the table.

At 3:41 p.m., according to my Batman watch, we officially reopened for business.

Our first customer was metal-mouthed Cooper Starr, the king of jerkdom.

"I'll take one cup of snot juice, if you please," he said.

He laughed like he had just told the funniest joke in the whole world. He waited while Maggie poured a cup. Her eyes nearly bugged out of her head when he slapped a ten-dollar bill down on the table. "Can you make change for a tenner?"

Of course we couldn't, but Maggie tried to figure it out, anyway, counting to ten on her fingers.

"Only babies count on their fingers," he snorted.

"Does it make you feel good to tease a five-year-old?" Luna asked.

"You bet it does," he answered. "This pipsqueak needs to close up shop right now. My brother, Pooch, runs the lemonade business on this street."

Cooper put the ten-dollar bill back into

his pocket, grabbed a handful of grass from the lawn, and was just about to drop it into our lemonade. He stopped when we heard a horn honking and saw a big white van rumbling down the street toward us. On its side, in large red letters, it said LOS ANGELES HOSPITAL.

"Cooper, your ride to the hospital for mutant research is here," I said.

The medical van pulled up in front of Viola Dots's house. The back doors swung open, and two emergency medical team members got out in a hurry.

"Watch out, kids," they hollered as they lifted a wheelchair from the van. "We got a sick lady coming through."

As they lowered the wheelchair onto the ground, I saw an old woman sitting in it. I gasped. It was none other than Viola Dots herself.

# CHAPTER 3

Viola Dots is one of the few people that Cooper Starr is afraid of. I've seen her chase him off her front porch, threatening to call his parents or even the police. The minute he saw it was Viola in the wheelchair, he took off running down the street. Luna and I dashed straight for her.

"Get your hands off me!" she was yelling at the medical team that was trying to help her.

"Just relax, ma'am, relax," a man with a beard said as they lowered her wheelchair onto the ground. "You've been in the hospital with a bad infection in your lungs."

"I told you," she squawked. "I'm much better now. I did not need a wheelchair for the ride here, and I certainly do not need one to take me into my own home."

"Just let us do our jobs, ma'am," the

woman who seemed to be in charge said.

"Let me up. I can walk," Viola shouted. "I know my rights."

The two medical workers shared a look. Viola Dots is a hard person to argue with. The one with the beard shrugged at his partner. His partner shrugged back, and they stepped away from Viola.

Viola got to her feet. "Well, it's about time," she said, whacking the bearded man in the arm with her purse.

"Ma'am, please!" he said. "If you don't settle down—"

"It's okay!" Luna interrupted, moving in between them and taking Viola gently by the arm. "We'll help Mrs. Dots inside. Won't we, Tiger?"

"Sure, let me just get my catcher's mask

so she doesn't whack me in the face," I said with a laugh. Luna frowned at me very hard. I guess this wasn't a good time for a joke.

"Good luck, kids," the bearded man said. "You got one spicy meatball on your hands."

He and his partner climbed back into the van and drove away. Before they left our block, I noticed that they stopped at Pooch's lemonade stand to buy a cup.

I checked my watch. The hour of power was almost upon us, and poor Viola was sick. It looked like there was going to be no fantastic-frame journey today.

Luna and I tried to guide Viola through the gate into her yard. She had to stop to cough several times.

"I don't need your help, either," Viola snapped at us, when she had caught her breath. "Chives will see me in."

This was not a good sign. It seemed she didn't remember that we had to leave Chives, her talking-pig butler, behind in the last painting because he had injured his leg. Her son, David, had stayed to take care of him.

"Don't you remember, Mrs. Dots?" I said very gently. "Chives is still in the art world, with your son, David."

"That Chives," she said. "He is never around when I need him. I could have used him to make me a cup of tea with honey.

That would fix this cough."

We were already inside the gate and heading up the path to Viola's house when it hit me: I'd forgotten all about Maggie and her lemonade stand.

"I'll meet you guys inside," I said and hurried back to my sister.

"I have to help Mrs. Dots now," I said, approaching Maggie. "Will you be all right on your own for a little while?"

"No," she said. "I don't have any customers. I still don't have any money."

"Have you learned that earning money is hard work?" I asked in my most grown-up voice.

Maggie nodded. I opened my mouth to point out how I gave up my invention time, so the world was not going to get to see my Pocket Buddy that day.

Then I had a thought. *Wait a minute. Maybe they could still see it.*

"I've got an amazing idea," I said. "Mags, this is going to solve all your problems."

I reached into my jeans and pulled out the prototype of the Pocket Buddy. "You can raffle off my invention," I said, feeling proud of how excellent a big brother I was being.

Maggie looked at me blankly.

"You know, a raffle," I said. "Like what they do at school when they want to raise money for the community garden? You give people tickets when they buy lemonade, and then pick a winner to get the prize,"

I explained. "Some lucky person is going to get the first-ever Pocket Buddy."

"Who would want this weird thing?" Maggie said.

"Oh, little sister," I said. "You have so much to learn about business."

I reached over and took Luna's sign off the table. Picking up one of the red markers, I wrote WIN A ONE-OF-A-KIND INVENTION. ONE RAFFLE TICKET WITH EACH PURCHASE.

I dashed into the kitchen and grabbed a sheet of paper. I wrote a list of numbers, from one to twenty-five, and ripped up the numbers into tickets. Running back to the stand, I told Maggie to just hand out a ticket with each sale, and that we'd pick the winner as soon as I got back. I took the

Pocket Buddy, polished it a bit with my shirt, and set it gently on the table.

"But I still don't have any customers," Maggie said. She looked like she was going to start crying again.

"You've got me," I said. "Now how about a lemonade? I'll buy one."

That made her smile. As she poured it, I dropped a dollar into the fishbowl and helped myself to a raffle ticket. Maggie looked very happy and gave me a big hug. I was mid hug when I heard Luna calling me.

"Tiger, get in here! We need you!"

There was panic in her voice.

I left Maggie and ran as fast as I could up the path to Mrs. Dots's house, not knowing what I was going to find inside. From the sound of Luna's voice, it didn't seem like it was going to be anything good.

# CHAPTER 4

Luna's head was poking out of Mrs. Dots's old front door. She looked very upset.

"Where have you been?" she asked.
"Mrs. Dots is a mess. She's coughing a lot.
I'm worried about her."

"Should I have my mom call a doctor?"
I asked.

"Viola refuses," Luna said. "She said no
doctors. She only wants us."

"*¡Ven aquí, niños!*" Viola called from the
living room. I could see her on her sofa,
lying down and sipping tea.

"That's Spanish," Luna said. "It means,
'Come here, kids.'"

We hurried into the living room. Viola
looked pale and weak.

"Look at my new painting," she said,
waving one thin arm in the direction of the
fantastic frame. "I finished it just before I
went to the hospital. I worked on it for many

days without sleeping."

"That's why you got sick," Luna said. "My grandma says you need to get eight hours of sleep every night."

"And eat fruits and vegetables," I added.

"I can feel my son, David, in this painting," Viola said. "It's as if he is speaking to me, calling for me. I'm old, children. And I've been ill. Who knows how much time I have left? I need to see my David."

I looked over at the huge golden frame, with its carved animals and ticking clock. The new painting was beautiful, like all the others Viola had done. It showed a girl with two braids tied with a purple ribbon, kneeling in front of a huge bundle of white flowers. I couldn't see the girl's face, only her back. The bundle of flowers was so big that it seemed like the girl was struggling to get her arms around it.

"Those flowers are calla lilies," Viola said. "And the original painting is called *The Flower Vendor.* It was painted by one of Mexico's greatest artists, Diego Rivera."

"My family is from Mexico," Luna said.

"I know." Viola nodded. "I've been practicing my Spanish, but it's still not very good. Your Spanish will be very helpful when we travel to Mexico."

"We?" Luna and I both said at once.

"Yes," Viola answered. "We are all going into the painting to find David. It's time."

"But you can't travel now," I said. "You've just had a bad lung infection. You need to get well."

"Don't try to talk me out of it." Viola put

her teacup down and sat up. "I'm going into the painting this time. And that's final."

"Mrs. Dots," Luna said. "You're too weak. You were just in the hospital."

"That's why I am coming with you," Viola said. With a great effort, she stood up. *Necesito a mi hijo.* I need my David."

"We'll bring him back this time," I said. "You don't need to go."

"You children say that every time, and what do you have to show for your promises?" she said. Her voice didn't sound mean, just sad. "My only son is still lost in the art world, and now my butler, Chives, is stuck there as well. I'm coming."

Viola started to cough again. Luna put her arm around her. Viola was coughing so loudly that at first I didn't hear what was happening.

Across the room, a clock began to chime. I looked over at the golden frame, at the clock mounted on the bottom. I saw the hand move. It was four o'clock, on the dot.

"The hour of power is starting. Quick, Luna!"

"Now, you stay put," Luna said to Viola, wrapping a blanket around her. "We'll be back with David. That's a promise."

Luna ran to me and grabbed my hand. We stood facing the painting. We heard a rip and saw a small hole beginning to open. We could feel the art world pulling us in, that feeling of suction. The real world around us grew dim and distant. The walls of Viola's living room began to fall away.

The hole in the painting grew larger. The familiar ripping sound became louder,

filling my ears. The living room rumbled; the floor shook. We weren't ready for this adventure. We knew nothing about Diego Rivera or his painting. And now Viola was counting on us to find David and bring him home before she got even sicker.

The hole in the canvas had spread to all the white flowers, and it glowed at the edges. The sweet scent of lilies wafted into the room. I felt the painting pulling us in, but I resisted. Something was holding me back. Then I heard footsteps, and I felt something heavy push us from behind.

The real world became a total blur. Colors swirled, thick and bold. Yellows, whites, and deep blacks. I clenched Luna's hand tightly as the heavy shape pushed us all the way into the other world.

What was that pushing us?

And then I knew. It was Viola. She was with us.

She grabbed my hand as we started to fall deep into the painting, through worlds and time. Her bony fingers clutched mine.

"*¡Ya voy, David!*" Viola yelled, as the three of us tumbled head over heels into the tunnel of time and space. "I'm on my waayyyyyyy."

# CHAPTER 5

It was a bumpy trip into the painting. My hand slipped away from Viola's and Luna's grasps, and I lost track of where they were. I landed with a thud onto red, dusty earth. The fall knocked the wind out of me. My body hurt, as if I had taken a punch right in the ribs.

Red-brown dust was swirling around me. I moaned, sat up, and looked for the others. All I could see was a wall of white calla lilies. I poked my head through the flowers and, looking down, saw the young girl from the painting. She had two black braids tied with a purple ribbon and large brown eyes. We were just a few feet apart.

When she saw me, the girl shrieked like she had seen a ghost. Before I had a chance to recover from momentary deafness, she jumped up from the ground. Dropping her large bundle of flowers, she ran toward a small red-clay building nearby.

"You scared her," I heard Luna say from behind me. Although Luna had landed in the flowers, too, she had tumbled into a patch of thorny bushes a few feet away.

"Not my fault," I said. "I'm sure she's never had a visitor from the future before."

I brushed the dirt from my eyes and looked around. In the distance, I could see the low buildings of a small village. The only thing nearby, other than dirt and trees, was the small red-clay building. It appeared to be a little shop that sold groceries and drinks. The girl ran straight into the shop.

A moment later, she reappeared at the doorway with a grown woman carrying a baby tied to her back with a blanket. I guessed the woman was her mom. The girl was pointing at us and talking in a frightened voice. When the woman with the baby saw us, she put her hand to her mouth.

But she didn't scream. Instead, she cupped her hands around her mouth and called, *"¡Héctor! ¡Ayuda!"*

"She's calling for help!" Luna whispered. "We should get out of here."

There was no time for that. The woman was running right toward Luna and me. To our surprise, she didn't stop. Her skirts rustled right past us.

"*Pobre abuela*," she said. "*¿Qué pasó, abuela?*"

"She's saying 'poor grandmother, what happened?'" Luna said.

We turned around and saw that Viola had landed in a patch of tall grass not far from us. She was clutching her leg, her face covered in dust. She was coughing. All the swirling dust had made her cough even worse. The woman with the baby had run to her side. She bent down and took Viola's hand, stroking her forehead.

*"¡Héctor!"* she yelled again. *"¡Ayuda!"*

An old man came from the little building. He ran to Viola's side, and together, he and the woman helped her sit up. The woman with the baby tended to Viola's hurt leg. The girl with the flowers held Viola's hand and smiled at her. Viola stopped coughing and smiled back. Then she closed her eyes to rest. The trip had been very hard on her.

Just then, a hand grabbed my shoulder. Startled, I looked up into a shadowy face that was almost hidden under a wide-brimmed straw hat.

"Hey, compadre," the face said.

I knew that voice.

"David!" I said, jumping to my feet. It was David all right, wearing a loose-fitting white shirt and sandals made of leather.

He looked like he fit in perfectly.

Luna hugged him so hard, I thought he was going to pop. "Viola knew you'd be here!" she said. "By the way, where is here?"

We all laughed.

"We're in a little village outside of Guanajuato," David said. "The people are really nice. The rice and beans are amazing. And Héctor over there is teaching me to play guitar. I was just coming for my lesson."

"How long have you been here?" I asked.

"Who knows?" David said. "By the way, Chives is here, too."

I looked behind David and saw poor

Chives trotting over to us on all fours, naked as the day he was born. His leg seemed healed, but his butler jacket was gone, as were his top hat and tie. Except for his orange color, he looked like any other pig you'd see on a farm. And he was not at all happy about that.

"Chives!" I said. "You look like a healthy pig!"

"Tiger means that in the nicest possible way, of course," Luna hurried to add.

"That is just the kind of insult I've had to put up with here," Chives said. "They treat me like an ordinary pig. First, they locked me in a filthy sty and fed me slop. They expected me to bathe in a mud puddle, can you imagine? Not this pig. No, sir."

"It's good to see you, Chives," I said. "Is

your leg all better?"

"My body is healed, but my spirit isn't," Chives said. "These people call me *puerco*, which means 'pig' in Spanish."

"But you are a pig," I said.

"They think I'm the kind of animal that is meant to be eaten." He snorted. "Luckily, David has protected me. He tells them I am his pet and leads me around town on a leash. Everywhere I go, people slap my rump. They don't know that I am a finely trained and properly educated butler."

While Chives was carrying on, I noticed David watching the three people surrounding Viola. "Who's that old woman?" he asked.

Chives squealed. "Mrs. Dots! My mistress is hurt!"

David gasped.

"Mama?" he whispered. "Could that be Mama?"

Chives sprinted over to Mrs. Dots's side. David didn't move a muscle. He just kept staring at Viola.

"Have I been in the art world that long?" he asked softly.

"Your mother said you've been missing for over fifty years," I answered.

"When I first got pulled into the fantastic frame, my mother was young, with black hair. She was strong and healthy. But now she looks so old. How did she get here?"

"She couldn't wait any longer for you to come home," Luna said to him. "She's sick.

She needs you. It will make her so happy to see you."

Luna and I stood together as David walked over to his mother. The others stepped aside and made a space for him. He kneeled down next to her.

"Mama," he said softly, taking off his straw hat. "It's me."

Viola opened her eyes and looked up. When she gazed at her son, it was like a mask had been lifted from her face. Her wrinkles almost seemed to disappear. Her eyes sparkled. Despite her pain, she pulled herself to her feet and threw her arms around David.

Viola and David held each other for a very long time, without saying a word. The flower girl came to us, and in Spanish asked

Luna what was going on. Luna replied in Spanish, and soon Héctor and the woman with the baby were gathered around her. They listened and nodded. When she was finished talking, Luna turned to me.

"I told them that David is Viola's lost grandson," she explained. "I said she had been looking for him for a long time, and now she's found him."

That was very good thinking. If Luna had said David was Viola's son, and that he had been lost in the world of art for over fifty years, those people would have thought we were making up a wild story.

At last, Viola let go of David and held him at arm's length, just looking into his face. She was smiling and crying at the same time. I didn't know you could do that. I looked at Luna and—can you believe it?— she was smiling and crying, too. So were the people from the village. It was a smiling-crying fest! The only people not crying were me and Chives, but that's mostly because pigs can't make tears.

"It's so happy and sad," Luna said.

"What do you mean?" I asked. "It's all good. They found each other. Now David can go home and help Viola get well."

Just then the baby on the woman's back began to cry. The mother tried to comfort the baby, but the crying grew louder. The woman looked concerned and ducked away into the shade of a tree. She untied the baby from her back, kissing it softly and holding it close. Luna went over to see if she could help. I saw her speaking with the mother, who was looking into her little one's face with sadness.

"Is everything okay?" I asked Luna when she returned to my side.

"It's not at all okay. That baby, whose name is Sofía, has something wrong with her eyes. And her mother, Señora Juárez, said a doctor told her Sofía will go blind if she doesn't get an operation very soon."

"Oh no," I said. "That's terrible."

"The family is too poor to afford the operation, but someone in town knows a doctor in Mexico City who might do it for free," Luna went on.

"That's good news, right?"

"Not exactly. The bus to Mexico City costs five hundred pesos."

"And they don't have that much money, right?"

"They're trying to get it. The girl with the lilies, that's Sofía's big sister, Antonia. She has been tending the flowers all week to take them into town on market day. That's today, but she has to sell all of those lilies to get enough money for the bus."

"That's a lot of flowers to sell," I said.

"It sure is," Luna said. "And she doesn't have much time. The bus for Mexico City leaves tonight at five o'clock."

Five o'clock. That was also the time we

had to leave, the end of the hour of power.

I looked at my Batman watch. It was 4:11 p.m.

"Are you thinking what I'm thinking?"
I asked Luna.

"That depends on what you're thinking,"
she said. But from the way she smiled,
I knew we were thinking the same thing.

"We have exactly forty-nine minutes to
help Antonia sell all those flowers before
we have to go home," I said.

"That's just what I was thinking," Luna
said. Her eyes shone bright as the sun. "My
grandmother always says that great minds
think alike."

"Your grandmother sure does a lot of
talking," I said with a chuckle.

"Tiger, there is a time and place for
jokes," she said. "And this isn't it. Forty-nine

minutes is not much time. And unless we want to stay here forever, we can't take even a second longer than that."

"Then why are you just standing there?" I said. "Baby Sofía is counting on us!"

# CHAPTER 6

We ran to the little shop, where Héctor had moved Viola into a chair on the shady front porch. She was alone with David, who was

bringing her a glass of water.

"Thank you, darling," she said, taking a sip of water.

I saw a look

of surprise cross Chives's face. As her butler, he had brought her thousands of glasses of water, but all she ever said was it was too cold or too hot or too full or too empty. The words "thank you" had never crossed her mind or her lips. But being with her son seemed to have changed Viola. She was suddenly as sweet as a doughnut hole.

Which, by the way, is my favorite part of the doughnut.

We explained Sofía's situation and how it was urgent that we try to help her.

"Oh, I wish I had brought my purse," Viola said. "I could have just given them the money they need."

"I don't have a cent," David said.

"Then we must try our hardest to help Antonia sell those flowers," Viola said.

"Okay," Luna said. "Everyone here is now on Team Sofía. Let's go make some money."

"If it's okay with you, I need to stay with my mother," David said. "She's in pain from her leg, and her cough is bad, but she says everything hurts less when I'm here."

I watched Viola smile at him and dab her eyes with a tissue. This was not the same person who just a little while before had been whacking a man with her purse.

"Chives, will you fill in for me?" David asked.

"With pleasure, sir," Chives answered in his best butler voice.

"Good," Luna said. "You can help us carry Antonia's flowers into town."

We got Antonia and divided the flowers, leaving her mother and Sofía at the shop.

We hurried down the dusty road toward the town center. Luna carried some of the lilies. Antonia and I did, too. We used Chives's leash to strap the rest onto his back.

It took a few minutes to get to the town plaza. It was filled with colorful buildings and crowds of people with animals, shopping and wandering around. I wasn't sure what year we were in, but there were a few classic-looking cars, so I knew it was the twentieth century.

"My snout is tickling." Chives snorted softly. "I think I may sneeze."

"*¿Qué?*" Antonia said from behind her flowers. "*¿El puerco habla?*"

"No, no, no," Luna said and slapped Chives on the rump. "Chives doesn't talk. He's a pig!"

But Antonia knew what she had heard, and she looked frightened.

"Tell Antonia that this pig makes a lot of annoying noises," I suggested. "But that just means he'll taste extra delicious for dinner."

While Luna translated my message, I whispered to Chives that if he didn't cool it, he might really wind up on tonight's dinner plate.

"That is insulting," he said, stomping his hoof.

Antonia's eyes grew even wider. I could see her trying not to scream. Without so much as a look back, she took off running. Just then, a man in all white walked out of what looked to be a butcher's shop on the edge of the square. His eyes went right to Chives.

"*Hola, puerco,*" he said with a gleam in his eyes.

"Eek!" Chives screeched and took off toward the town square at a fast trot, dragging me after him.

We made quite an entrance into the plaza. It was market day, and the square was lined with stalls selling everything from tortillas to pottery to flowers. Every building was painted in different glowing colors: banana yellow, sky blue, cherry red.

"Whoa, Chives!" I yelled, pulling on the leash and taking the flowers off his back. "You have to calm down or you'll scare away our customers."

"What customers?" he answered. "There are a lot of flower stalls here. Why would anyone want to buy our flowers?"

He was right. There were many stalls selling flowers of all colors and sizes.

We searched the square, but we couldn't find Antonia. It was crowded with people shopping, playing instruments, and watching their children run around.

"Antonia!" Luna called, but there was no answer.

"I told you that you shouldn't talk in front of her," I said to Chives. "Now you've freaked her out. And we have no idea where to look for her."

I checked my watch. It was 4:23 p.m. Thirty-seven minutes left until five o'clock.

This was not good. We had so much to get done and so little time. We had to find Antonia, and fast!

# CHAPTER 7

We wasted three precious minutes looking for Antonia. We zoomed around and finally found her in a far corner of the plaza. She had put her flowers down and was offering them to people passing by.

"Look!" I said when we spotted her. "Antonia has customers!"

A man and woman had stopped in front of her. She handed the man a lily, and he gave it to his girlfriend. Then he reached into his pocket for a coin.

"Way to go, Antonia!" Luna said.

We scooted across the plaza, but just before we reached Antonia, a group of boys ran to her from out of nowhere. One of the boys flashed the man a big smile while the others led his girlfriend to the opposite side of the plaza, where they had a large flower stall with a fancy sign. They handed her a bouquet of colorful flowers.

"They stole her customers!" Luna screamed. "They can't do that!"

"But they did," I said. "Just like Cooper and Pooch. Bullies are bullies, no matter where or when they live."

"I have something to say about that," Chives said.

Before we could stop him, he trotted right up to one of the flower bullies.

"*Hola, puerco,*" the boy said to Chives, slapping him on his rump.

Chives rose up on his hind legs until he was face-to-face with the bully.

"May I have a word with you?" he said.

When the bully heard Chives speak, a look of fright flashed across his face. He took off running, with Chives close behind.

Antonia was busy gathering the flowers back into her arms.

She had tears in her eyes, just like Maggie had when Pooch ruined her lemonade stand. Except that if Antonia didn't sell her flowers, her baby sister might go blind. The stakes were a lot higher than Shop-Cool dolls.

"What can we do for her?" Luna said.

"Maybe we should split up," I suggested.

"That could work," Luna said. "Those kids might be able to bully one person, but they can't stop us all. We'll each take a bundle of lilies and go to different corners of the square. We can outsell them."

"I'll find Chives and keep him with me," I said. "He's not safe. I noticed at least two butcher shops in this plaza."

Luna explained our plan to Antonia, and we divided up the flowers.

"Okay, Tiger," Luna said. "Here's the deal. Each flower costs ten pesos. Many of the young men like to buy them for their girlfriends. All you have to do is hold up the flower and say, *'¿Para su novia?'* That means, 'For your girlfriend?'"

I repeated the words. It felt good to be able to say something in Spanish.

"If you are selling a flower to an older person, hold up the lily and say, *'Para su casa,'* which means, 'For your house.' Got it?"

"No problem," I said. "I could do this in my sleep."

"We have to hurry," Luna said. "What time is it?"

I checked with Batman. According to him, it was 4:30 p.m. We had a half hour to sell the flowers, get Sofía and her mom on the bus, and go back to where we arrived.

"Okay, if we sell every one of these flowers, we'll have the five hundred pesos we need," Luna said. "We'll meet back here in ten minutes. It'll be tight, so hurry. Remember, we have to be back by five o'clock. On your mark, get set, go!"

Luna and Antonia took off in separate directions. I hurried to the bully's flower stall and found Chives hanging out in front. He had scared off all the boys there.

"Like all bullies, they were cowards at heart," Chives said. "A few words from a talking pig, and they scampered away like scared rabbits."

"Good work, Chives. Now we have to sell these flowers fast. I just wish I were better at selling things."

"Confidence, sir," Chives said. "That's what it takes to succeed in business."

With his snout to my back, Chives nudged me into the crowd.

"Over there," he said, leading the way to a gray-haired woman.

*"¡Hola, señora!"* I said, holding up my lilies. She shook her head no and quickened her step, but I remembered Luna's words.

*"¿Para su caca?"* I said with a smile.

The lady looked shocked. Her eyes bugged out. She shook her finger in my face and let out a long, loud

stream of Spanish. It was clear I had made her angry. She stomped away.

"The words you were looking for are *'para su casa,'*" Chives said. "That means 'for your house.' You said *'para su caca.'*"

"I said *'caca'*? Uh-oh. Does *caca* mean what I think it means?"

"Unfortunately, it does, sir. Potty talk sounds the same in every language."

I was so embarrassed. Any shred of confidence I had went down the drain. To make things worse, I had wasted four minutes. And I still hadn't sold one flower.

I had told Luna I could sell these flowers in my sleep.

I was wrong. I couldn't even do it wide-awake!

# CHAPTER 8

I was not about to give up, not with Sofía's future in my hands.

"There's a possible customer over there," Chives whispered and motioned to a man by the fountain. He was gazing at a pretty woman sitting alone at a café.

"Now repeat after me," Chives said. *"Para su novia."*

*"Para su novia,"* I repeated. "For your girlfriend."

"Confidence, sir," Chives said, nudging me forward.

I approached the man and held out the lily. *"¿Para su novia?"* I asked, trying to sound sure of myself.

The man looked my way and smiled. He gave me a nod.

"Ten pesos," I said, holding up ten fingers. The man reached into his pocket. I was about to make a sale. He handed me the silver coin, and I handed over the lily.

*"¡Ay!"* He gasped as he grabbed the flower stem. I looked down and saw that the bottom of the stem was jagged and uneven. It hadn't been cut well. The stem had scratched his hand where he grabbed it.

"Pardon!" I said, hoping that that sounded something like *sorry*.

I took the flower back from him. Reaching into my pocket, I pulled out the second Pocket Buddy prototype I had taken from my house. I flipped out the scissors and trimmed the flower stem so it was smooth. The man glanced down to see what I was doing. When he saw my Pocket Buddy, he let out a long whistle.

"*¡Guau!*" he said. "*¿Qué es esto?*"

Though I don't speak Spanish, I could tell by his voice that he was impressed with my Pocket Buddy. I showed off some of its features, even turning on the tiny FM radio.

He laughed and slapped me on the back many times. Then he shook my hand and slapped me on the back some more. Usually, I love it when people admire my inventions. But I didn't have time for all this praise. My Batman watch said 4:37 p.m. It had taken me three minutes to sell a single flower!

"This is going way too slowly," I said to Chives. "There has to be a faster way. I wish I could invent a flower-selling device."

I pressed on my forehead, hoping I could knock a good idea out of my brain. Then I felt it. The answer was right there in my hand.

My Pocket Buddy! I could raffle it off. It had worked for Maggie. Or had it? I didn't stay around long enough to find out.

Maybe it had been a giant flop. Or maybe it had been a big hit, and she had made a big pile of money. There was one way to find out.

It was time to change up the game.

# CHAPTER 9

"Chives, go get Luna and Antonia," I said. "Make sure they bring all their flowers. Trot like you've never trotted before!"

He hurried off as fast as his stubby pig legs could carry him, and I went into action. I grabbed two buckets from an empty stall and put them on the ground in front of me. Then I found an old wooden board behind one of the stalls and placed it across the buckets.

Next, I needed paper. I searched my jeans pockets and came up with an old spelling test I had forgotten to have my parents sign. Too late now! I tore it up into little pieces. Using the pen from my Pocket Buddy, I wrote out numbers from one to twenty-five on the little slips of paper.

When Chives returned with Luna and Antonia, I climbed up on the wooden board that I'd placed across the buckets.

"Tiger, what are you doing?" Luna asked.

"No time for questions," I told her. "Just translate. And talk loudly. We need to attract a crowd."

"Ladies and gentlemen," I yelled like
one of those guys at the county fair who are
trying to get you to toss Ping-Pong balls into
fishbowls. "May I have your attention?"

Luna stood by me and hollered in Spanish
into the crowd. Only a few people turned.

"It's not working, Tiger," Luna said. "They
don't care."

Chives looked up at me with a sly squint
in his piggish eyes.

"You can't send a boy to do a pig's job,"
he whispered.

Without waiting a heartbeat, he sucked
in air and let out the loudest, most eardrum-
shredding squeal you've ever heard.
Everyone in the plaza stopped what they
were doing and stared at him. When he had
their attention, he stood up on his hind legs,

faced the crowd, and took a long and stately bow. The crowd applauded and gathered around us.

"They're all yours," Chives whispered.

All eyes turned to me. Suddenly, I felt very confident. I had an invention in my pocket that I truly believed in. I couldn't sell flowers, but this I could sell!

"Ladies and gentlemen," I cried. "My name is Tiger Brooks, and I am the grandson of the world-famous inventor Thomas Edison."

Luna stopped translating and gave me a look when she heard that part.

"Just play along," I whispered to her. "It's for a good cause."

"I have come all the way from America," I shouted, "to share my amazing invention."

I took the Pocket Buddy out and held it up in the air.

"I present to you the Pocket Buddy, an all-purpose tool to serve your every need. It has a pen, a pair of scissors, a magnifying glass, and a spork. What is a spork, you ask? It's a combination spoon and fork. The eating tool of the future!"

Luna translated, and the crowd seemed impressed, but I was just getting started.

"Best of all, you can use these tools while listening to your favorite tunes."

I pulled out the antenna and flipped on the radio switch. A bouncy dance tune wafted into the plaza, and the crowd cheered.

"We are giving you the opportunity to own this one-of-a-kind invention by joining our raffle," I shouted. "All you have to do is buy one of Antonia's beautiful calla lilies. Ten pesos each. Your money will go to help her baby sister, Sofía, get the eye surgery she desperately needs. Step right up for your chance to win!"

A huge line formed immediately, with people shoving and pushing and holding their pesos up in the air.

All three of us worked together to handle the rush. Luna took the money, Antonia

gave out the flowers, and I handed out the raffle tickets. Soon we had sold every one of the calla lilies. Luna's palms were filled with pesos. She handed the money to me, and I carefully placed it in my pockets.

The crowd was calling for the raffle to begin. I looked at my watch. It was 4:48 p.m. That meant we had exactly twelve minutes to do the raffle, get Antonia and her family to the bus, and get back to Viola and David in time to return home.

This was going to be tight.

I reached my hand into the pile of tickets and swished them around, trying to build up the drama. It worked. In fact, it worked too well. When they saw my hand reach for the tickets, people in the crowd started to buzz with excitement. One thing was clear: They all really wanted to win. The noise got louder and louder.

"Quiet down, everyone," I said. "There can only be one winner. Let's all stay calm."

Luna translated, but no one wanted to hear what she said. All they wanted was to win. The crowd started chanting. Normally, I would have been happy that my Pocket

Buddy was so popular, but instead, a wave of worry shot through my entire body.

We didn't have a minute to lose. After the raffle, we would need everyone in the crowd to clear out so we could get back to Viola and David.

I swished the tickets one more time until my fingers found the one. Slowly, I pulled it from the bucket.

*I hope this goes smoothly*, I thought. *Please be calm, everyone.*

The crowd was chanting. I looked up, took a deep breath, and read the number out loud.

"Number fifteen!" I called.

"*¡Número quince!*" Luna echoed.

My heart was beating so fast and so loud, I couldn't hear the crowd's reaction.

# CHAPTER 10

A gasp of disappointment went up in the crowd as everyone turned their heads to look for the winner. Nobody was coming forward to claim the prize.

Finally a tiny voice cried, *"¡Número quince! Aquí."*

The crowd parted. A boy, eight or nine years old, was holding his ticket up in the air. When the crowd saw who had won, they burst into a cheer and hoisted the boy up onto their shoulders. They carried him to the front, chanting his name.

*"¡Miguel! ¡Miguel! ¡Miguel!"* they cried. Then they chanted other things that I didn't understand.

"They're saying he is the town's kid genius," Luna said to me. "He invents all kinds of stuff and goes around fixing everyone's radio."

I grabbed the Pocket Buddy, my only remaining prototype, and handed it to Miguel. I confess, it was hard to give it up. But at least it would go to someone deserving, a fellow science kid. I hoped that someday in the future, Miguel would invent something amazing himself.

We inventors have to stick together.

We left the crowd chanting Miguel's name and ran from the plaza. It was six minutes to five. As we reached the dusty road out of town, we came across a group of boys gathered there. I recognized them as the boys from the flower stall. They stood in a line with their arms folded, blocking our way.

The one in the middle cocked his head and stepped forward. He said something to Luna in Spanish. It didn't sound friendly.

"He wants some of our money," Luna said, looking worried.

The leader of the flower-bully gang took another step forward.

"*¡Ahora!*" he said, reaching out his hand.

"What's that mean?" I asked Luna.

"It means 'now,'" she said. "But I don't care what he says. He is not getting Sofía's money."

"Pardon me, Miss Luna," Chives whispered. "Perhaps this requires a butler's skills. May I handle this for you?"

"Do your thing, Chives," Luna said.

Chives stepped forward to face the bullies.

"*Hola, puerco,*" one said with a smirk.

Chives smiled and took a few steps toward the large mud puddle in the middle of the road. With a sudden mighty squeal, he jumped into the mud, stomping and snorting like a pig having a meltdown. Mud flew everywhere. The bullies put their arms up, trying to protect themselves, but stumbled and fell into the puddle. Chives yelped in delight, kicking mud all over them.

"Run!" he cried to us.

We took off down the dirt road, our feet practically flying. As we came closer to the shop, we heard hooves behind us.

"I'm a pig, and I love it!" Chives screamed.

It was three minutes to five when we arrived back at the shop. We were winded and panting, covered in mud and sweat.

Things were almost exactly as we'd left them. Viola was resting in the shade, her foot propped up on a bamboo chair. Señora Juárez was serving her a cold fruit juice. Viola was holding little Sofía on her lap, while right next to her, David and Héctor were playing guitars and singing.

"*¡Mamá!*" Antonia cried, as she ran up to Señora Juárez, her palms filled with pesos. "*¡Mira, Mamá! ¡Mira!*"

When Señora Juárez saw the money, she screamed and lifted Antonia into the air and

hugged her with all her might.

"You did it!" David cried, putting his guitar down and giving us high fives. "Now little Sofía has a chance to get her surgery. We were hoping for this moment. Señora Juárez is all packed. The bus leaves in just a few minutes."

"Then they better hurry to the bus stop," Luna said. "They can't miss it."

"I'll take them," David said. "It's not far. Just up the road."

"There isn't time," I said. "We have to be back exactly where we landed in two minutes."

"Then we can all go home," Luna said. "All of us."

David and Viola were strangely silent.

"We've decided . . . ," David began. "I

mean, we've talked it over and . . ." He couldn't go on. Viola handed the baby to Señora Juárez and put her hand on David's shoulder.

"I'll explain," she said. Then she stood up, tall and healthy looking. "David and I are not coming with you. We are going to stay here, in Mexico."

"What?" I cried. "But the whole point was to bring you two safely home."

"You've got to come back with us," Luna said. Tears began to form in her eyes.

"I've lived in the real world long enough," Viola said. "This is where I want to be. In the world of art. Here there is no time. My cough is gone, and my back is as strong as it was when I was young. And I will remain the same age as I am now. I can be with

my son for as long as we'd like. We have so
much time to make up, don't we, David?"

David wrapped his arms around her.
"There's a small farm next to Señora
Juárez's that is empty," he said. "Mama and
I are going to live there. We'll farm the land.
Mama can paint the fields and the hills.
And Héctor is going to teach me guitar."

"Who knows?" Viola said. "My David

could be a musical genius, one day, if he practices."

"Is this what you want, David?" Luna asked.

"We'll have a good life here," he said.

"A life filled with fresh air, good friends, good food, and as much color, art, and music as we like," Viola said.

"Can we come visit you?" I asked. I felt a lump in my throat, the kind you get when you're trying not to cry.

"Perhaps from time to time," Viola said. "And if we want a change, you can always place a different painting in the frame. Or Chives will do that task. That is, unless you would like to stay here with us, Chives."

"No, Madame," Chives said. "I must go back where I belong, where I have a proper wardrobe. I'll look after the manor, see to it that the house stays in decent shape but spooky enough to keep away the curious."

Antonia pointed at Chives and laughed.

*"¡Sí! ¡Sí!"* she said. *"El puerco puede hablar."*

"Yes, the pig can talk," Viola said to Antonia. "And bathe. Which I suggest you do at once upon your return, Chives."

Chives smiled and bowed. "On my honor, Madame."

"Wipe your tears, everyone," David said. "This is a happy ending."

David stretched out his arms for a great big hug. We all held one

another tightly. It was hard to separate, but we knew we had to. As we took our positions, I felt the real world pulling on me, that suction I had come to know.

"Goodbye," I said. "We'll miss you!"

# CHAPTER 11

I felt Luna take my hand and squeeze it tightly. From the corner of my eye, I saw David take Sofía in his arms and head down the road with Señora Juárez. But it was like I was looking through the wrong end of binoculars. The art world seemed far away, our connection to it growing more and more distant. I saw Viola waving goodbye, just before she disappeared entirely.

"This is not the end, children," we heard

her call. "The world of art is never-ending and everlasting."

All at once, the red, sandy earth faded away, and we felt ourselves falling.

"Farewell, Madame!" Chives called as he tumbled with us through time and space.

The journey home was the most peaceful

one we'd been through—except for when Chives snouted me pretty hard in the back.

We landed gently in the real world, floating into Viola's living room through Diego Rivera's beautiful painting of Antonia with her calla lilies.

"We made it," Luna said, climbing to her feet.

"Indeed we did," Chives said. "And look at this house. What a mess; not up to my standards at all. I'll get the vacuum as soon as I've finished my bath."

He trotted off toward the stairs. Then he paused and looked back at us.

"Perhaps tomorrow afternoon, you can stop in for a spot of tea?" he said. "I'd like that very much."

And with that, he went up the stairs.

Luna and I just stood there in silence, taking in all that had happened.

"Is Mrs. Dots truly in there?" I asked, pointing to the fantastic frame. "Forever?"

Neither of us knew the answer.

"It's so quiet in here," Luna said.

It was quiet inside, but outside, I heard a clamor of voices. It was the same type of commotion we'd heard in the village plaza.

"Maggie's raffle!" Luna said. "We still have to help her."

"You think those people are shouting for my Pocket Buddy?"

"Of course!" Luna said, grabbing my hand. "We've seen it happen before! People are people, no matter where they live."

Outside, a rowdy crowd was gathered around Maggie's stand, everyone holding up their tickets. There must have been thirty people there. Kids, grown-ups, even Pooch. Maggie's fishbowl was filled with dollar bills.

"Hey, Mags," I called. "You need help?"

"I got this," she said. Where was my sad little sister now? In the hour we were gone, Maggie had turned into a confident,

calm, clever little businessperson. I guess that's what a great invention like the Pocket Buddy will do for you. Give you confidence. It worked for me, and now it had for her.

"Everyone be quiet or no one gets the prize," she said in her bossy voice. When everyone was silent, she reached her hand into a bucket and pulled out a ticket.

"Number nineteen," she cried. "It's got a name on it, too, but I can't read the letters."

"Someone should teach that little squirt to read," Pooch yelled, throwing his ticket.

"You're just a sore loser," another person said. "The kid did a great job. And by the way, I'm number nineteen."

It was Simon, our neighborhood mail carrier. He was holding the winning ticket. Maggie handed him my Pocket Buddy as the crowd gathered around to check out his prize.

"You're rich," Luna said to Maggie, looking at all the money in the fishbowl.

"I'd bet there's forty bucks in there," I said. "You could buy four dolls with that."

"I don't want Shop-Cool dolls anymore," Maggie said. "Instead, I'm going to buy a big new set of tools, so I can be an inventor and get really famous. That's my dream. I want to be just like you, Tiger."

"That is the sweetest thing to say," Luna said to her.

It was sweet, but Little Mags had a long way to go before she could become an inventor. She didn't even know what a voltage meter was. Or a circuit board. Or a screwdriver, for that matter.

But then I thought, if I can travel through a magical frame into the world of art, then maybe Maggie can learn to be the inventor she dreams of becoming.

After all, the one thing I've learned from my adventures inside the fantastic frame is that anything is possible.

# CHAPTER 12

For two weeks, Luna and I didn't really talk about our art adventure in Mexico or the hour of power, or David and Viola. We were still best friends who walked to school together and hung out all the time, but

neither of us brought up our secret lives as art explorers. It was almost as if we didn't want to face the fact that all of our amazing adventures were over.

Then one day, our art teacher announced that our class was going on a field trip to the Norton Simon Museum in Pasadena, a town very close to our school.

I hadn't ever been to that art museum.

On the day of the trip, a guide took us through all the rooms, pointing out one beautiful painting after another. We passed a still life of fruits. A landscape of a river and leafy trees. A group of ballerinas in fluffy skirts. And a portrait of a woman with the longest neck you've ever seen.

"And now," our tour guide said, "we come to one of our museum's most prized

pieces: Diego Rivera's famous painting *The Flower Vendor (Girl with Lilies)*."

Luna and I looked up, and there she was on the wall. Antonia, her braids tied with a purple ribbon, holding her huge bunch of calla lilies.

"That painting is so boring," Cooper Starr said, crossing his arms. "It's just a girl with braids sitting there with—"

"You don't know what you're talking about, Cooper," I blurted out. Before I knew what was happening, I had walked up to the wall and stood in front of the painting.

"There's a lot to see in this," I said. "You might not see it at first. Art doesn't work that way. You have to really look at it and soak it up. And think about the painting, with your heart and your brain. Don't you wonder who this girl is? And why she's carrying so many flowers?"

"No," said Cooper. "Why would I care about that?"

"Cooper Starr!" our art teacher said. "I've warned you all morning. Now I'm done warning you. You obviously don't know how to behave in a museum, so go back to the bus and wait there until we're done."

"But there's nothing to do there, and it smells like salami sandwiches," he whined. "And the bus driver has this hairy mole on his cheek."

"Have fun staring at it," I said to him. "We'll be staring at beautiful art."

After he was led off, Luna and I asked our teacher if we could spend one more minute looking at the Diego Rivera painting.

"Of course." She smiled. "I'm happy you love this painting as much as I do."

When we were alone, Luna and I looked at the painting closely.

"Do you see that?" I said, pointing to a little spot on one of the flowers.

"See what?" Luna asked. "I just see flowers."

"Look again," I said. "Right there, in the center of the flowers."

"Oh, I see it," Luna said. "At least I think I do."

"Luna, I think it's moving. I bet it's Viola, waving at us from inside the painting."

Luna squinted hard.

We moved closer to get a better look.

"Excuse me, kids," the guard said, tapping us on the shoulders. "You can't get that close to the paintings. Sorry, you have to step back."

When we had backed up, we looked at the painting again. The spot was gone.

"I saw it," I said. "It was her, saying hello."

"Maybe," Luna said. "Or maybe it was just our eyes wishing it was her. I hope Viola and David are happy there."

"I know they are," I said. "It's hard not to be when you're surrounded by beauty."

Luna smiled and took my hand, and together we walked through the museum, letting ourselves soak up the beautiful world of art.

# ABOUT THE PAINTING

## *The Flower Vendor (Girl with Lilies)*
## by Diego Rivera

*The Flower Vendor (Girl with Lilies)* was painted by Diego Rivera in 1941. It shows a girl kneeling in front of a large bundle of calla lilies. We cannot see her face because she has her back to us. She has two braids tied with a purple ribbon. The two braids tell us that she is a young woman who has not yet married.

What we notice first about the painting is the size of the bundle of flowers. It is so big that there is no way the girl can carry it herself. The title of the painting tells us that she is taking the flowers to market to sell them. But how will she carry them? How can such a young girl carry such a heavy load?

Diego Rivera loved to paint the common people of his native Mexico. He painted peasants who worked on farms and lived in villages. He painted workers in factories whose labor helped build the country. He wanted to create art that reflected the lives of the working people of Mexico, not the rich people.

Diego Rivera was born in 1886 in Guanajuato, Mexico. When he was only three years old, his parents caught him drawing on the walls of their house. Instead of punishing him, they hung chalkboards and canvas all over to encourage him to keep drawing. By the time he was ten, he was enrolled in art school in Mexico City. As a young man, he spent ten years studying art in Europe and became friends with many of the great artists of the twentieth century.

When he returned to Mexico in the 1920s, his paintings changed. He didn't want them to be enjoyed only by well-educated people who could afford to buy them for their homes. He thought that art should be enjoyed by everyone—especially poor, working people. He began to paint large murals for public buildings in Mexico City. His art celebrated the native people of Mexico, their ancient customs, and their traditions. He became a leader in what is now known as the Mexican mural renaissance.

Diego Rivera has been criticized for using his art to express his political beliefs. The idea that was most important to him was his belief in the dignity of the ordinary working person. When we look at *The Flower Vendor*, we can see the strength of a young girl who is struggling to make a living by taking her flowers to market.

Diego Rivera died in 1957 in Mexico City. He was married several times, but his most famous romance was with the great artist Frida Kahlo. Together or separately, they are known as two of Mexico's most famous and respected artists.

Just like in this book, *The Flower Vendor* hangs in the Norton Simon Museum in Pasadena, California.

# ABOUT THE AUTHOR

**Lin Oliver** is the *New York Times* best-selling author of more than thirty books for young readers. She is also a film and television producer, having created shows for Nickelodeon, PBS, Disney Channel, and Fox. The cofounder and executive director of the Society of Children's Book Writers and Illustrators, she loves to hang out with children's book creators. Lin lives in Los Angeles, in the shadow of the Hollywood sign, but when she travels, she visits the great paintings of the world and imagines what it would be like to be inside the painting—so you might say she carries her own fantastic frame with her!

# ABOUT THE ILLUSTRATOR

**Emily Kimbell** fell into illustration by accident and stayed there because it was a good excuse for not going to parties. She also works as a character and background artist for animation and in her spare time she likes to spend time in places where there are trees.